Oscar Fay Adams

The Presumption of Sex and other Papers

Salzwasser

Oscar Fay Adams

The Presumption of Sex and other Papers

1. Auflage | ISBN: 978-3-84604-892-4

Erscheinungsort: Frankfurt, Deutschland

Erscheinungsjahr: 2020

Salzwasser Verlag GmbH

THE

PRESUMPTION OF SEX

AND

OTHER PAPERS

BY

OSCAR FAY ADAMS

AUTHOR OF "THE STORY OF JANE AUSTEN'S LIFE,"
"DEAR OLD STORY TELLERS," "POST-
LAUREATE IDYLS," ETC.

BOSTON
LEE AND SHEPARD PUBLISHERS
10 MILK STREET
1892

THE AUTHOR

TO

HIS DEVOTED FRIEND

J. Albert Brackett

The author takes this occasion to express his obligations to the publishers of the North American Review, who have kindly allowed him to reprint in this volume the copyrighted articles from their pages entitled " The Mannerless Sex," " The Ruthless Sex," " The Brutal Sex," and " Our Dreadful American Manners."

Felton Hall,
Cambridge, Mass., January 25, 1892.

CONTENTS

INTRODUCTION

✳ ✳ ✳ ✳

IT is the vice of a great deal of popular criticism that it rushes to hasty conclusions and rests its judgments upon assumptions instead of basing them on discriminating comparisons. Several months ago I was led to write and publish in the *North American Review*, one of the papers included in this volume entitled *The Mannerless Sex*. The article was the outcome of a good deal of observation on my own part, with added testimony derived from the observation of many men and women whom I have known in various localities. Nothing was farther from my intention than an " attack upon womanhood," as the paper was termed in some quarters. On the contrary, I felt that although much, if not the greater part, of what I wrote had been said before, it yet needed to be reiterated; and feeling convinced that what I was about to say was true, I said it. Moreover, the paper being but a brief one, imposed limitations upon me, and constituted but a part of what I purposed saying. Later, I followed this article by others on *The Ruthless Sex* and *The Brutal Sex;* and in the present volume I have added to the discussion some words on *The Vulgar Sex* and *The Presumption of Sex.*

But a host of critics, assuming that I had in the first-named paper said all that I intended, at once began to pass judgment upon it, — judgment which misinterpreted, in the majority of cases, the scope of the author's intention. A few there were who looked at the subject from all sides, as a critic should, and troubled themselves very little about the writer's personality. Such persons occupied themselves with considering whether what I had said was true or false, and, if true, whether it were wise to insist upon saying it in the manner I had done. But critics of this stamp were not many. The majority, after quoting from what I had said, declared that I was cynical, one-sided, and what not, and ended by stigmatizing me as " ungallant."

But what had gallantry to do with it at all ?   Is the preacher ungallant who creates a sensation in the pews by preaching against the sin of idle gossiping indulged in by the women of his congregation ?   As a matter of fact, his denunciations are not sufficiently inclusive, for gossip is not the sin of one sex alone ; but he is not ungallant.   Nor is the judge ungallant who passes sentence upon a female criminal.   Both preacher and judge are laboring in the interests of reform ; and why should the writer be styled ungallant who endeavors, however imperfectly, to call attention to a reform which it seems to him that women should set on foot. Unwise he may be, his generalizations hasty, and his denunciations too sweeping, but he is not necessarily ungallant.

But what is meant by being gallant? The dictionaries interpret the phrase as displaying courtesy to women, for one thing, and as living incontinently, for another. Now, the essence of courtesy is not flattery, as some would have it, neither is it an excess of candor at all times and in all places. The man who rushes up to a woman, all unregardful of circumstances, to declare a shortcoming which he fancies he has detected in her, is ungallant, we must admit. But the writer who calls attention in print to certain errors and mistakes committed by women in their daily intercourse with men and with each other, can hardly be placed in the same category. His manner may be open to criticism, but it is unfair to credit him with other motives than the hope of helping towards the reform he thinks is desirable. Unlike the man in the first instance, he does not single out an individual as the object of his criticism, but leaves it for individuals to determine whether or not his remarks apply to them. And to speak of him as "ungallant" is simply to beg the whole question.

If I had been at all in doubt regarding the wisdom or expediency of having spoken out in meeting as

I did in the paper on *The Mannerless Sex*, the number of approving letters I received from persons in widely separated localities would have reassured me. The most of these were from women who were large-minded enough to look at the matter dispassionately, and to acknowledge that what had been said by me was needful to be said.

Nor was this all. I have been many times assured by women in social gatherings that I had said nothing but what was true; that they had often seen with regret the things I had adversely commented upon, and that they wished to thank me for uttering my protest.

Assurances like these naturally had far more weight in determining

me to follow out my original intention of discussing another side of
the feminine character, and of com-
menting with at least equal plain-
ness upon some of the failings of
my own sex, than the bestowal
upon me of such epithets as " rude,"
" ungenerous," and " ungallant,"
mingled with hints of the social
ostracism which I should have to
dread.

When a second paper appeared
there was the same amount of hasty
judgment passed upon it as had
been made upon its predecessor;
but the publication of a third, called
The Brutal Sex, induced a change
in the attitude of some of my critics.
Certain of these, who were unquestionably feminine, hailed the

article as an evidence that I was trying to regain the favor of the sex I had "maligned" by "abusing" my own, as they kindly phrased it. Other critics, finding their estimate of me as a misogynist disturbed, were inclined to rank me as a cross-grained cynic in general,—a conclusion as ill-founded as the other. And both classes of censurers were concerning themselves with something quite aside from the main issue, which was not the personality of the writer and the nature of his motives, but whether or not he had spoken truly and wisely, so hard is it to discuss a subject without first surrounding and obscuring it with a personal atmosphere.

The present volume is issued in

furtherance of my original intention of saying, regarding each sex, some things that I felt needed to be said. I do not claim for them the merit of originality, but I do claim for them honesty of intention; and while we average men and women remain the imperfect beings that we are, I have no fear that they can be said too often.

THE PRESUMPTION OF SEX

THE PRESUMPTION OF SEX

* * * *

SAID one of the brightest of American literary women to me in the course of conversation not long ago, —

"I want men to give up to me in everything. I want them to yield to me even when I am in the wrong, because I am a woman. It is a man's duty to sacrifice himself for a woman always."

It was playfully said; but the speaker meant much of what she affirmed, and a majority of women would have agreed with her. Her attitude was that of most women in civilized countries. Woman, in general, cares very little about the abstract truth of any subject under discussion, but much, very much, for the spirit of personal deference manifested in the yielding of her masculine opponent in obedience to her insistence. That the matter at issue may remain just as it was before does not concern her. She fancies that she has gained a victory if she wins assent; and so she does, for she gains all she has been contending for.

Her present position is a perfectly natural one, and one for which man is primarily responsible, however he may dislike it. When women were treated as grown-up children, and the possibility of rational discourse with them commonly denied, it was as simple a matter to assent to their assertions, where masculine authority and comfort were not in question, as to say, " Yes, dear, if you will be good," to the child who asks if he may have a piece of cake. An external deference which cost nothing was paid by man in exchange for a constant practical acknowledgment of his superiority.

Now that women in our day have over and over again proved their ability to meet men successfully in argument, the liking for conquest, irrespective of the merits of the case, remains almost as strong as ever; and for a man to maintain his point and show no signs of yielding, would be considered as an affront by the greater number of women. No matter how courteous in argument the man may be, it avails him nothing if he withhold that crowning flower of courtesy, assent.

"It is ungallant to contradict a woman," runs the woman's creed, and contradiction means the maintenance of opinions opposed to their own.   But, as was said before, man has himself to thank for this state of things.

When more material matters than arguments are considered, and precedence and deference are accorded to women, such precedence and deference have their origin in the respect and careful consideration paid to weakness by generous strength all the world over. That women should presume at times upon such deference, and persistently exact it, is not surprising, though certainly unpleasant to witness. So long as the world stands, it is to be hoped that men will not fail to show such deference and courtesy to women as should be paid by the strong to the weak; but the millennium will not have arrived until all women shall have ceased to demand it.

A curious example of the presumption of sex, as manifested by women, is shown in the attitude of the larger number of those who claim that women should be enfranchised. I am very far from arraying myself against that movement, but I am not prepared to believe that the immediate results would be as beneficent as is often urged. We are told that the extension of the suffrage to women would be the opening of a new era in matters social, municipal, and political. We may concede this fact, but would the " new era " be in all respects in advance of the present one?

Woman says it would, and declares that her influence is purifying and uplifting whenever it is allowed to penetrate. Something like a Golden Age is promised if she be permitted to vote. Now, setting aside the question of her abstract right in this matter, it by no means follows that wrong is going to be at once made right by her acquirement and exercise of the franchise.

To begin with, her perception of the rights of property is at present but dim and vague. Witness the course of the temperance crusaders a few years ago.

Intemperance is a blight upon the country; therefore, let us destroy the property of the liquor dealer : so ran their logic.

An inability to perceive but one moral truth at a time, or but one aspect of it even, causes women to commit grave mistakes, to create abuses even greater than the one which they endeavor to do away with, when grappling with complex moral problems. Take, for example, the social evil. When the question comes up regarding the licensing of houses of ill-fame, and by such action preventing their increase beyond a certain number, and subjecting the inmates of the licensed houses to strict and constant medical supervision, women exclaim in horror. " What! set the seal of municipal approval upon such a sin ? " they cry. They will not be convinced, as men are, by the logic of facts. And what is that logic? Simply this : that it is hopeless to expect, in our time, the utter extirpation of incontinence. This being the case, two courses are open for adoption. One is the licensing in each town of as few houses of resort as possible, and the subjecting these to frequent medical supervision and inspection, in order to guard against the spread of disease. The other course is to attempt to make men virtuous by act of parliament, and endeavor with greater or less success to suppress all such houses. What follows the adoption of the latter course? In some places, spasmodic attacks of public virtue, during which such houses are raided by the police, and then let alone for long intervals; in other places, where the suppression is most effective, an increase of illegitimate births results in more than one grade of society.

In the treatment of the subject there must be a choice of evils. Looking at but one aspect of it, the matter of licensing the evil *seems* the worst of the two, and so most women would consider it. Regarding it from all sides, there is certainly something to be said in its favor while we are limited to a choice of evils. Not until the average man is far less vulgar and brutal than at present, not until he has risen to the plane on which incontinence shall be as abhorrent to him as it is to most women, may we look for ideal treatment of the question in modern life.

I instance these two subjects of the social evil and the rights of property as affording, in the light of past experience, room for doubt of woman's superior handling of them if the power to vote in relation to them were given her. In time, no doubt, she would learn to look at the larger aspect of moral questions without in the least abating her horror of sin and crime ; but I cannot think that putting the ballot in her hands would result in such a rapid setting straight of the crooked things of this world as many ardent and noble women reformers believe.

Another instance of woman's presumption of sex is shown by some feminine writers in a certain glorification of women apart from and above men. One sees it in anthologies of " women poets " and " women writers." Herein the writings of women are valued apparently quite apart from their relation to literature in general. It is only as the work of women that we are besought to heed them. That the sex of the writer should be a matter of any moment to the reader, except as so far present in the writer's mind as to visibly color his or her words, is something that man in general finds it difficult to apprehend. Yet this " sex-piety," as it has been called, constantly appears in the work of some women, and, whenever found, is detrimental to literary excellence.[1]

---

[1] At the Philadelphia Exposition, the work of women in various departments of industry was exhibited by itself in a Woman's Pavilion, and it is proposed to repeat this absurdity at the Columbian Exposition in 1893. Will women never learn that the completed results of skilled labor in any direction are of interest and value *because some skilled brain or hand has produced*, not because they are the work of either sex ? Such a setting apart of woman's work *because* it is woman's work is more than foolish — it is a sin against true canons of judgment.

But if presumption of sex is a noticeable failing in women, it is still more observable in man. Not every man would allude to himself as one of the lords of creation, but nearly every man secretly thinks of himself as such. And if this attitude of man is unpleasing to woman, she has had her part in producing it. But I am not so sure that it is disliked by her. It amuses her at times, I am inclined to think, and by a deft word here, a smile of approval there, she contrives to strengthen man in his own estimation, well aware that she thus best furthers her own aims.

As each loyal British subject was once firmly convinced that every true-born Englishman was the physical superior of at least twenty frog-eating Frenchmen, so is every man of the opinion that women are a distinctly inferior race of beings. As a matter of sentiment, however, each man excepts his mother from the fact of general inferiority, for being *his* mother, she must needs be out of the common at the very least.

Now, whether the belief rests upon adequate foundation or not, its acceptance leads to several results. One of these is to give men a contempt for feminine capacity in all but a very few directions. Until within the last thirty or forty years women accepted this contempt as quite natural, and believed implicitly in their own lack of capacity. Witness the narrow range of studies deemed proper for women to pursue till within a comparatively few years. Note the testimony afforded on this point by all but the most recent literature of English-speaking peoples, to go no further. But for man's deeply rooted belief in the superiority of his own sex in everything but child-bearing, and, according to Mr. Craig, woman performs that in a poor, makeshift fashion, the human race might have been much farther advanced than it is to-day. His persistent effort to confine woman to what he interprets her sphere to include has hindered his own development quite as much as it has retarded hers.

From his disbelief in the capacity of woman springs his habit of condescension to woman's supposed intellectual level. I can conceive of nothing more galling to a woman of average intelligence than to have a man adapt his subjects and his treatment of them in conversation with her to a distinctly lower plane of thought than his own, instead of talking to her in the same sensible fashion that he would converse with another man. Not until a man sees that he is talking over another man's head does he place his speech upon a lower plane. He always pays his masculine hearer the implied compliment of possessing an intelligence equal to his own; but nine times out of ten he insults his feminine hearer by the assumption that because she is a woman therefore she is a fool, or very near it. That women endure and forgive, or at least excuse, such insults, says very much for their good-nature under great provocation.

From his inward conviction of his own superiority, man is led to believe that such qualities as bravery and fearlessness, for example, are more especially apparent in him. He ridicules the feminine dread of a mouse, which he miscalls fear — quite another sensation, by the way; but in the front of real danger he sometimes fails to make as good a showing as his sister woman, whom, indeed, he has been known to trample upon, in his efforts to secure his own safety. Moreover, when endurance of pain, or even discomfort, is concerned, he frequently comes far short of the example set him by woman. He boasts that his is the stronger sex, and asserts its greater powers of self-control. How does he display his greater capacity for self-mastery?

In more or less profanity — a habit of speech from which he debars woman, although with her inferior powers of self-control she ought, it would seem, to be allowed a larger freedom than his in this particular.

In his more frequent use of intoxicants. But if he, with his superior powers, finds it difficult to keep from excess in the use of liquors, he ought to consider similar excess on the part of woman a venial offence on account of her general inferiority. Yet he insists that the weaker creature shall be kept to a higher standard than he sets for himself in this regard.

In his almost universal incontinence. The maintenance of his physical welfare being, in spite of his superiority of sex, impossible to preserve without a violation of the laws of chastity, he allows himself the widest liberty in this respect, and denies equal or indeed any freedom of conduct to woman, his physical inferior.

In summing up this matter of the presumption of sex, it would seem as if woman's presumption carries with it less harmful results than man's.

It is oftentimes amusing, sometimes annoying, but is seldom attended with such grave consequences as his. Man's presumption of sex being more firmly implanted in his nature, becomes a part of himself, something he cannot get away from. The perfectionists, holding that they had attained to such a plane of goodness that they could commit no sin, very soon fell into evil ways. Man, believing above all things else in his own superiority, loses his sense of the true relations of men and women to each other, becomes dictatorial and condescending by turns, a tyrant and a flatterer as the mood takes him, and self-indulgent when his vices are concerned.

Not until men and women cease

to glorify their respective sexes and leave off taking themselves in this respect seriously, as it were, and meet together not merely as men and women, but as equal intelligences in all essential matters,— not until then can we expect fair judgments of one sex from the members of the other.

THE MANNERLESS SEX

THE MANNERLESS SEX

✳✳✳✳

PERHAPS it were best to say at once that woman is referred to under this title, that the reader may not remain for a moment in doubt which sex is meant. The phrase, " the gentler sex," is, I consider, a most misleading one as applied to women, and I have been led to assume as a result of my personal observations, that the title given to this paper is, on the whole, the one most purely descriptive of woman.

I am very well aware, that to

declare an absence of good manners in woman is to run most decidedly counter to received opinion on the subject; but I maintain that this same " received opinion " is founded on a basis that is largely imaginary. The world has been told for so long a time that it is woman who supplies the restraining, softening, and refining influences which are at work in human society, that it has in great measure come to believe the assertion most implicitly, even in the face of a strong current of testimony setting quite the other way. Men believe it, or affect to believe it, from considerations of gallantry. Women believe it without question.

It is my purpose here to assert

that, however great an influence may be exerted in behalf of the conservation of manners by exceptional women, the statement that woman in general is the refiner of manners is, in any large sense, an utterly false one. Furthermore, I have no hesitation in declaring that the code of manners followed in public by the average woman is disgracefully inconsiderate, superlatively selfish, and exasperatingly insolent: such a code, in fact, as would not remain in force among men in their intercourse with one another for one half-hour.

Regarding the rudeness of women in their intercourse with the world at large, I shall refer, in passing, to a few forms of it which have doubtless forced themselves upon the attention of very many persons who can readily furnish illustrations drawn from their own experience:—

First, The indifference with which a woman will contemplate the fact that the convenience of others has been sacrificed to her caprice. Very observable in *young* women.

Second, The needless delay a woman often causes in making her appearance when visitors have called upon her. Most commonly noticed among women who are no longer classed as girls.

Third, The unwillingness of a woman to wait for another person to finish speaking before beginning to speak herself. A characteristic of nearly all women.

Fourth, Woman's failure to recognize the importance of an engagement. This is most noticeable among women who have the fewest social duties.

The rudeness of women to men is, for reasons which will be sufficiently obvious to the discerning reader, less common than that of women to each other, but it is too frequent to be suffered to pass without comment in this place.

The behavior of women in the street-cars has received in certain particulars rather more attention than I think it has deserved. The charge has often been brought against women that they have ac-

cepted seats in the cars without
acknowledging the courtesy of the
men who rose up to accommodate
them ; but so far as my observation
goes, the charge is not wholly borne
out by the facts, although the man
who has given up his seat usually
fails to hear the acknowledgment,
in his haste to escape to the car
platform.   Something might be said
against the custom practised by
many women of entering a car filled
with men, and relying on the gallantry of the occupants to give up
their seats, instead of waiting for a
car offering better seating capacity ;
but until railway authorities provide
better accommodations, it will not
do to be strenuous on this point.
Much more might be justly said

against a favorite custom with many women, which consists in delaying an open car for several moments, while they debate which one of two or more shall enter the car first. What does it matter to them if the persons upon the car are in haste to get to their destinations? They have the satisfaction of knowing that every one on the car has lost one or more minutes by their sense-less, amiable wrangling.

Let us look at a more flagrant instance of woman's rudeness to-ward her fellow-man. We will sup-pose ourselves at a railway station, in which a number of men are in line before the ticket window. A woman enters, and, instead of taking her place at the foot of the line, goes at once to the front and informs the agent that she wants a ticket to Evercreech Junction, by way of East Cato. Sometimes she adds that she is in a great hurry. She either can not or will not understand why she is sent to the foot of the line, and when she arrives before the ticket window again, she becomes voluble over her grievance, and, after securing her ticket, remains to ask a number of questions, the answer to any one of which she might learn from the railway time-table she holds in her hand, or from the porters at the train doors. That persons are waiting behind her whose time is presumably as precious as her own is nothing to her, and, if asked to make room for the next person, she is over-whelmed by what she terms his impertinence.

There is not a person who reads this who cannot recall similar scenes, I am very sure. At the post-office, or in any other place where the invariable rule is " first come first served," woman endeavors to re-verse this rule in her own favor, and, failing to secure this reversion at times, she invariably sets down the fact to man's lack of gallantry.

Towards men of a rank which woman considers beneath her own, she is often shamefully inconsid-erate or shockingly impertinent. I have more than once in English railway stations seen porters, while staggering under the burden of

heavy trunks, stopped by women
who kept them standing several
moments, while they put to the
unfortunate victims questions which
would much better have been asked
of the station master or of unem-
ployed porters close at hand.   But
what of that?   It is the duty of
porters to be civil when questioned,
no matter what Atlas-like load is
crushing their shoulders.   Then,
too, I have witnessed American
women browbeating persons whom
they termed their " tradespeople,"
in a manner which would have re-
sulted in their being knocked down
had they been men, and which made
one regret the desuetude of the
ducking-stool which they richly deserved.

It were useless to multiply instances in illustration for this part of my subject. To put it briefly, a very great number of women in their relations with men presume upon the privileges of their sex, the degree of presumption depending very often upon the rank of the persons with whom they are brought into contact.

Perhaps the most common example of the ill-manners shown by women to each other is the habit, in which they seem to take much delight, of saying spiteful little things to one another. Du Maurier has lately satirized this trait very cleverly. The sisters Tiptylte are represented in his drawing as taking a sociable cup of tea with their friend, Miss Aquila Sharpe. On their informing her that they mean to attend Mrs. Masham's fancy ball as Cinderella's ugly sisters, wearing false noses on that occasion, Miss Sharpe commends their plan as most excellent, and adds, " But why false noses ? " The artist's satire will not be called exaggerated by any one who has noted the un-feeling, spiteful onslaughts with which most women diversify their intercourse with one another.

But it is when fair woman goes a-shopping that she becomes least admirable. Then her hand is raised against every woman who crosses her path. From the moment that she pushes open the swinging doors of the first retail shop she enters, and lets them fly back into the face of the woman behind her, till she reaches her home again, she has laid herself open at every turn to the charge of bad manners. She has in her progress made tired clerks spend hours in taking down goods simply for her amusement, when she has not the smallest intention of purchasing from them. She has made audible comments upon " the stupidity and slowness of these shop-girls." She has swept off from loaded shop counters with her draperies more than one easily damaged article, which she has scorned to pick up and replace. She has jostled against other women and met their indignant looks with a stony, not to say insolent, stare.

She has needlessly blocked the way when others wished to pass her. She has carried her closed umbrella or sunshade at an angle that was a perpetual menace to any woman who came near her. She has put up her glass and stared haughtily through it at the gown of the woman next her at the bargain-counter. In her shrill, penetrating voice, she has discussed in the most public places gossip reflecting more or less injuriously upon other people. She has, in short, done very little that she should have done, and very, very much that she ought not to have done; yet she returns from it all with a serener conscience than a mediæval saint coming home to the convent after a day particularly well filled with meritorious deeds. She will complacently tell you that a man can never learn to shop like a woman. And man can never be too thankful for his inability in this particular direction.

It is needless labor to recount in detail instances of woman's rudeness to her fellow-woman. They can be supplied from the reader's own experience in numbers great enough to justify the truth of the assertions here made, and I have no desire to dwell at length on the subject.

I do not mean to be understood as declaring in broad terms that man is mannerly while woman is not, for I observe with regret in many of my own sex an indifference to the rudimentary courtesies which

is fatal to their reputation for good
manners, and I recognize in many
women a watchfulness for the rights
of others, a gentleness in the assertion of their own, that deserve a
respect little short of veneration.
What I do insist upon, however, is
this: that in public the average
woman shows an inconsiderateness,
a disregard for the ordinary courtesies of existence (which amounts
sometimes to positive insolence), to
a degree which is not anywhere
nearly approached by the average
man.

The reason for this difference in
the behavior of men and women
I do not propose here to discuss.   I
will not say, for instance, that man
is altruistic and that woman is self-

ish, because I do not believe in any such putting of the case. But I leave for others the task of pointing out the causes of this difference between men and women, and indicating, if they will, the remedy for the present state of affairs, and content myself in this place with a brief presentation of the subject, in the hope that its healthy discussion may induce a reform in the public manners of our sister-woman.

THE VULGAR SEX

THE VULGAR SEX

****

IN the course of a short walk along a city street, not long ago, I passed in succession a number of persons who might not be inaptly taken as representing in Hogarthian fashion the progress of the average man from the borders of infancy onwards. The first whom I met was a handsome little boy of four years, dressed *à la* Fauntleroy, and looking as sweetly innocent as it is possible for childhood to appear. After him came a well-dressed boy of eight or nine, who paused to sketch, after the ancient Pompeian fashion, some indecent figures on a house wall. Two schoolboys of fourteen or fifteen stopped to look at him for a moment, and then passed on, one of them relating to his companion some indecent jest suggested by the rude drawing. The next persons I encountered were a couple of youths of eighteen or nineteen, both of whom were doing their best to cover the pavement with tobacco juice, and liberally adorning their conversation with oaths between whiles. Their loud tones could still be heard not far distant, when two well-dressed men, whose ages might have been anywhere between twenty and thirty, approached me. It was evident that they were not only men of fashion, but fairly intelligent as well. They were unquestionably born in the purple, and knew it. And equally apparent was it that they were of the earth earthy, and that they did not know it. As they drew near I could hear what it was they were discussing with such seeming relish. It was "The Clemenceau Case," which they had attended the previous evening. Not far behind these came two prosperous-looking men in middle life; and as they were passing me, I heard one of the men say to the other, " By the way, you ought to drop in at (naming a certain prominent house of ill-fame much frequented by aristocratic patrons). There are some new arrivals there quite worth your while."

The innocent child first seen was the type of what all these who had followed him had once been. The thoughts called up by what I had observed in my walk were not to be easily put aside, unpleasant as they were. All too vividly I saw how, in all human probability, the shades of the prison-house would begin to close about the child, and his likeness to those who followed him deepen as years went on.

Whatever may be said in praise of tobacco, and it has inspired many a worthy pen, too much, I think, cannot be urged against a use of it which results in defiling our pavements, street-cars, and every public

place, except the church, with tobacco juice, and vulgarizing hotel
corridors, offices, legislative halls,
and even private houses, with that
greatest indignity offered to the
fictile art, the cuspidor. And it is
the vulgar sex that. is responsible
for such a state of things. Woman
has never experienced a personal
need of the cuspidor, and tolerates
its presence near her only as a pro-
tection from a greater vulgarity. I
am not saying that the use of
tobacco is a vulgar thing; but I do
most distinctly aver that the use of
it by the average man, if judged
from its unpleasant and too familiar
consequences, is unmistakably vulgar. It is vulgar ignorance that
causes the laboring man with a quid

of tobacco in his mouth to become
a nuisance to every cleanly person
about him. It is vulgar indifference, a much graver offence, that
puts the man of education, be he
legislator, college professor, or
doctor of divinity, in the same attitude towards his nearest fellow-
beings. Reform in this, as in other
matters, must work from the top
downwards, and perhaps, if we look
back far enough, we may see some
signs of reform in this regard; but
the particular evidences of it are not
strongly apparent in our streets and
other public places. But offences of
this character betoken a surface vulgarity only; it is when we note the
evidences of vulgarity of mind that
the average man appears least
admirable.

It may be asserted, in theory at least, that the entrance into life of the human being, and all which most nearly appertains to the reproduction of the human type from the union of the sexes, constitute a subject which should be treated, whenever it is discussed, with feelings not far removed from the deepest awe and reverence. Most women do by nature thus regard it; and where they do not, it is because of masculine influence exerted in a contrary direction.

Man but rarely considers the matter so seriously. On the contrary, the average man is disposed to regard it with the utmost levity. From the time he enters the primary school the sacred mystery of birth is for him the theme of endless jests, the unfailing topic for coarse and obscene tales. Vulgarity for him begins almost with the closing of the nursery doors upon him, and ends only with life. If the boy is of the lower ranks, he becomes familiar with the vulgarity of grown men long before his teens are reached. If he be of a higher class, he finds out a few years later that the smutty story, the witticism turning upon sexual matters, is as popular with men as with boys. A youthful De Maupassant, expelled from school for writing obscene verses, very naturally develops into the De Maupassant who in maturer life replaces the coarsely sensual themes by suggestive allusions and refines upon vulgarity with the utmost charm of style. There is a distinction to be drawn between vulgarity and coarseness. Coarseness of mental fibre may be the fault of one age, and vulgarity of feeling that of another. In "the spacious times of great Elizabeth" names were named and words were bandied about in common talk that, as Thackeray remarks, "we should screech now to hear mentioned;" but I very much question if, in essentials, our more nicely spoken age is not more vulgar than that one, even with the three centuries given for the advancement of the race. The men of Shakespeare's day had not made very much progress towards refinement of speech in regard to sexual matters, but they are not therefore to be accounted vulgar. They were coarse, and brutally so, we may think, but vulgar they were not. Vulgarity, in its essence, is the characteristic shortcoming of our age, which outwardly professes to admire decorum and delicacy, yet is always ready to lend, *sub rosa*, a willing ear to the broad jest, the *double entendre*, and the obscene tale. Now and then a man of the Shakesperean age, strangely devoid of reserves, appears among us. Such a man is Walt Whitman, moving about amid a generation which has refined its native coarseness into vulgarity, and cries out that he is coarse. He is of kin, in certain respects, to Marlowe,

Massinger, Ford, and the others of
that coarse-fibred, but by no means
vulgar-minded, company, and is to
be judged by the same rules that we
judge them. It is not his fault that
he has been placed in the wrong
century.

One important distinction between the men of the past and
those of to-day is in relation to
these matters. The men of the
sixteenth century honestly considered sexual topics to be as legitimate subjects for the exercise of
their talents in ordinary conversation
as any other, and consequently they
spoke of cuckolds, strumpets, and
marital infidelities generally with as
little hesitation as we allude to
our fingers and toes. The men of

the nineteenth century shun such themes in *general* conversation, but at other times are as prone to discuss them as are sparks to fly upward. Our distant ancestors felt no shame in talking as they did, and saw no reason why subjects like these should be reserved for a corner; but we profess a shame which we do not feel, otherwise why should we banish such themes at most times, but make merry over them in the smoking-car, the club, or the bar-room?

But we are fearful of shocking the sensibilities of our womankind! So if we be Frenchmen we resort while in the society of women to the *double entendre*, and the delicately veiled allusion to the forbid-

den theme; and if we be English-
men or Americans we sedulously
avoid, when with women, all refer-
ence to the matter, but roar with
laughter over the broad jest or the
ingeniously salacious tale when we
are out of their company.

We are not at all afraid of shocking ourselves, yet in the nature of
things there is no reason why we
should not guard the awesome fact
of human birth, and all relating to
it, as reverently as woman is disposed to do. There is no reason
why man should treat it with vulgar
levity any more than woman does.
If a broad or obscene jest appears
by accident in the columns of a
reuptable newspaper, a thrill of
horror seemingly runs through the

community; but, nevertheless, the newsboys cannot sell that particular number of the paper fast enough to meet the demand. The nearer a journal can approach to the handling of tabooed subjects without actually crossing the line, the greater its popularity. The boundary between what may, and what may not, be said in print is constantly advancing towards latitude in this respect.

In general literature the tendency is the same as in journalism. When the refined sensuality of *Laus Veneris* first appeared all England was seized with a spasm of exceeding great virtue ; but it turned the leaves of its Swinburne all the same, and when later and even more daring worshippers of the erotic muse came forward, the public scarcely deigned to be shocked at all. Now that Swinburne has given bonds to respectability, there are those who declare that his strength has departed, heedless of the fact that his wondrous mastery of words and music is as firm as ever.

It is the fashion to sneer at the British Matron and the American Young Person, and the unreasoning temper of the one and the unsophistication of the other have without doubt exercised at times an influence not altogether beneficial upon the literature of the Anglo-Saxon race. Prudishness has occasionally taken the place of vigor, but still, to the existence of these much-derided individuals we owe the fact that our literature is not, like that of some other nations, as broad as it is long. To them we owe it that we have a Tennyson, a Scott, a George Eliot, a Mrs. Oliphant, and a Howells to set over against a De Musset, a De Maupassant, a Zola, a Balzac, and the Goethe of the Elective Affinities.

It was said not long ago that the literature which was not fit and proper for women of matured intelligence to read, if they desired, was that which was concerned with criminal court proceedings and the investigations of the dissecting-room; and no man who is not a specialist needs to read such literature as this either.

Why should the majority of us who are not profound students of human nature, but only men who want to be entertained, instructed, and, it may be, elevated — why should we turn with such relish to the coarseness of the past, to the vulgarity of to-day? Where one man reads the dramatists of the seventeenth and eighteenth centuries, as a student of human nature, with an honest desire to know how our distant ancestors thought and felt, and what manner of men they were, a hundred men read them for their coarseness, remaining blind all the while to their real and great dramatic excellence.

Similarly, where ten men read De Maupassant for the matchless charm of his style, a thousand read him in the hope of finding *risque* passages somewhere along his pages.

If we turn from dramatic litera-ture to the modern acted drama, we find that here, too, the average man prefers the vulgar to the intellectual and the elevating. If a play is known to deal in a peculiarly sug-gestive way with forbidden topics, men of all social grades flock to the theatre to behold it. The church continues to oppose the theatre upon grounds no longer tenable, and thereby reduces its influence in this respect to little or nothing. If it ever learns to discriminate be-tween forms of dramatic art which appeal to the higher intellectual faculties and those which minister only to the vulgar taste that sees in sexual relations merely material for coarse levity or refined sensual amusement, and, so discriminating, condemns only what ought to be condemned, it may hope to accomplish something of worth in this direction, but not otherwise.

Women have not been as alive in the past to their responsibilities in regard to the theatre as they should have been, and they now find it possible to sit calmly through plays which a decade or two ago they would not have dreamed of attending. Their powers of effective remonstrance are very much circumscribed, it is true; but if women were to refuse to accompany their husbands and lovers to plays which they know to be objectionable in general tendency, a certain measure of reform in the drama would follow. And to thus refuse need not be interpreted as being prudishly afraid of hearing something improper. On the contrary, refusal should be taken as expressive of the honest aversion that every woman naturally feels to hearing the most sacred of human experiences handled with careless and vulgar irreverence.

That the average man does not feel this same aversion is his misfortune, though it is not probable that he will ever feel it to be so. But taking him as he is, let us see how he is the gainer by his callousness.

In the first place, he has a wider field for the exercise of his wit. More than half of the jests and witticisms of the world turn upon matters relating exclusively to the physical relations between the sexes.

In the second place, he has opened to him a wider range for his imagination. The poet, unhampered by conventionalities, may chant the praises of Venus as loosely as he pleases, and is always sure of finding enthusiastic listeners under the rose. The novelist, similarly unfettered, may revel in sensual descriptions that leave nothing unsuggested, but are suited to tastes that do not require literal phraseology to add to their enjoyment. Now, these are unquestionable advantages, if we look at the subject from the standpoint of one who has no regard for the advancement of humanity. On the other hand, by his want of delicacy in these matters, the average man loses the capacity for making correct moral estimates. The greatest mystery of life cheapens in his handling. To him the healthily pure becomes dull and commonplace — a thrice-told tale that has lost all relish to his ears.

These are disadvantages that in the life of the race must weigh heavily in the scales against the gains we have mentioned. There are men, and not a few, who are as free from taint of vulgarity of every kind as it is possible for poor human nature to be; and there are women, not a few, who are hopelessly vulgarized; but when all is said, these are exceptions in each sex, and it is masculine influence which has helped to blunt the edge of woman's sensibilities wherever that edge has been lost.

Not until the average man of one grade turns with distaste from the literature of the *Police Gazette*, not until the average man of a higher grade has ceased to delight more in the darker pages of the elder dramatists than in the pages that are fairest, not until men of all ranks, clerical and lay, from laborer to bishop, from shop-clerk to poet, cease to derive enjoyment from the cleverly told but questionable story, the witty but smutty jest— not till all these things have come to pass, can our sex hope to lose the title of the Vulgar Sex.

THE RUTHLESS SEX

THE RUTHLESS SEX

****

F there is one more characteristic difference than another
between man and woman, it lies, as
has often been noted, in the manner in which any adverse criticism
directed against either sex is regarded by the members of the particular sex supposed to be aspersed.
If it happens to be the feminine sex
upon which the remarks have been
made, our sisters arise as one woman
to defend themselves. And why ?
Simply because each woman feels
that *she* is individually attacked,

that *she* is at fault, that the writer or speaker is aiming directly at *her*. On the other hand, if it be the masculine sex which is criticised, man, as a general thing, pays little or no attention to the matter. Generalities, he has found by experience, hurt no one in particular. No man's individual vanity is wounded by what may be said in disparagement of his sex as a whole.

Passing from the sex to the individual, we find a different state of affairs. If in the intercourse of social life some woman is harshly criticised, do her sisters at once rally to her defence? Very seldom, it must be confessed. Instead, the word of disparagement is echoed very faintly by a few women, very distinctly by many more, and with a delicate ingenuity in the prolongation of the note of dispraise worthy of admiration from a purely artistic point of view. Let a man be disparaged or harshly spoken against; do we find, as a rule, his brother-men, those who know him well, uniting to swell the chorus of adverse speech? I think not. Indeed, it is a well-established fact that men in their intercourse with one another display a chivalrous regard for their fellows, to a degree almost unknown among women. The loyalty to individuals which flourishes so vigorously amongst men, seldom finds its counterpart among their sisters. It seems to me that it cannot be a hard matter to decide which is the loftier attribute of our nature — the feeling of personal loyalty to individuals of a sex which is due to a tolerant attitude of mind, or the fierce loyalty to one's sex which has its root in individual vanity and self-love. There are men who delight in stoning him who is down, as, on the other hand, there are women whose spirit of charity shown in behalf of other women in similar situations is little short of angelic; but the sexes, in the order named, are not largely made up of such members. In spite, then, of some exceptions either way, the broad, distinctive fact remains that, as a rule, men are loyal to their fellows, however carelessly they may view any attack upon their sex; while women are disloyal to their sisters individually considered, but quickly resentful of any slight, real or supposed, which may be placed upon their sex.

One result of the persistency with which women make personal application of general assertions is a perpetual air of being on the defensive, which manifests itself often in the adoption of a pitiless code of judgments passed mentally, or otherwise, upon those about them. This of itself would not establish the truth of the assertion that women are more cruel than men, but it certainly has some force as an argument upon that side of the question.

It may seem a false putting of the case that such an assertion should be made, .when the many works of charity and mercy in which woman is engaged are remembered; but in spite of these labors of women the fact remains relatively true. Says Ruskin: "There is not a war in the world, no, nor an injustice, but you women are answerable for it; not in that you have provoked, but in that you have not hindered. . . . There is no suffering, no injustice, no misery in the earth, but the guilt of it lies with you."

Indifference, according to Mr. Ruskin, is the sin of which woman is most guilty — an indifference which arises from that narrow habit of mind which is exclusively occupied with the present moment, which refuses or is unwilling to grasp any other than the purely personal aspect of it. Her sympathies are quickly roused to what is immediately before her eyes, *to what no mental effort is required to perceive,* — as, for instance, a horse savagely beaten by its driver, — but it goes no further.

Suppose that we are riding upon a street-car and the horses are straining every nerve to pull the heavily loaded car up some sharp rise of ground. A street corner is reached, and a woman standing there signals the driver to stop his car for her convenience. Unless he has received positive orders not to stop while going up hill, he obeys her

(with considerable inward grum-
bling), and the horses, which have
stood their ground with some dif-
ficulty during the delay, are forced
to redouble their exertions in order
to overcome the inertia resulting
from the stopping of the car. That
she could have signalled the car
from the foot of the hill or from the
top never occurs to the woman,
who, desiring to get on at that
especial point, has no thought of
anything further, the pain and even
suffering which she has occasioned
the horses being a matter of no
moment to her. Or, supposing the
car is not ascending an up-grade,
but is moving along upon a level
stretch of road when signalled to
stop at a street corner. A few

steps farther on a woman stands waiting for the car to come exactly opposite to her. It does not seem worth while for her to walk those few paces and get on the car at the point where it has stopped for the convenience of others, and thus save the horses which draw it the strain and discomfort of an extra stoppage. Here are instances of her indifference resulting in cruelty. Such occurrences as these cited are not exceptional, as any person who has occasion to travel on street-cars knows, but are happening hourly on every horse-railway line. And the average woman never perceives that anything is wrong in her practice in this regard until some one else, usually a man, has told her of it. She acknowledges that she never thought of it before, and forgets all about it by the next time she gets on a car.

I might instance other examples of cruelty resulting from woman's indifference, but those already named show the general character of those I have in mind. I pass on now to speak of a more flagrant kind of cruelty, springing from another cause. Miss Helen Gray Cone, in her poem, "The Tender Heart," describes a young man, who is devoted to hunting, as so wrought upon by the pathetic pleading of a girl, who quotes at length from the poets against the sin of killing the fowls of the air and the beasts of the field, that —

" At Emerson's ' Forbearance ' he
Began to feel his will benumbed;
At Browning's ' Donald ' utterly
His soul surrendered and succumbed.
' O gentlest of all gentle girls,'
He thought, ' beneath the blessed sun ! '
He saw her lashes hung with pearls,
And swore to give away his gun.
She smiled to find her point was gained,
And went, with happy parting words
(He subsequently ascertained),
To trim her hat with humming-birds."

It is not very long ago since the cry went up that certain species of birds were in danger of speedy extinction from the wholesale warfare made upon them in the interest of milliners and their customers. A few women, be it said, had always by voice and example protested against a fashion which demanded such a sacrifice of animal life for its gratification; but it was not until men had almost unanimously exclaimed against it that even a partial reform was accomplished. I fear there is very little reason to believe that, if fashion should again demand a sacrifice of birds, it would not be offered by a large majority of women till vigorous remonstrance on the part of the other sex induced another reform. But why should not women in general perceive the cruelty of such a fashion as quickly as men, and, not waiting to learn gentleness and mercy from the so-called rougher sex, exclaim against it immediately? Is it not because vanity supplements indifference, in this case, with cruelty of the most unnecessary, indefensible kind as its consequence?

To pass to wider aspects of the question. Women have endowed charities — that some man has founded. Nay, they have sometimes established hospitals themselves, but not until man has pointed out the way. All honor to the Elizabeth Frys and humble Sarah Martins, but it was a John Howard who preceded them. The order of the Sisters of Charity was founded by a man !

It has happened not seldom in the history of the world that women have directly held the reins of empire. How does the record of their rule compare with that of monarchs of the other sex ? Did Boadicea, Mary Tudor, Elizabeth, and Catharine of Russia display in their reigns any such marked qualities of gentleness and mercy as would be sufficient to distinguish them as pre-eminent for the possession of those qualities above their brother sovereigns?   Were those women who ruled by proxy, like Eudoxia, Catharine de Medici, and the brilliant and scandalous array of women who pleased the sensual fancies of the second English Charles and the fifteenth French Louis, renowned for their merciful attributes?   All these held for a time the destinies of whole peoples in their hands, but we do not hear that they exercised any restraining influence over savage men, but in one most notable instance quite the contrary.   And the queens of the ancient world —

do they seem to have hated cruelty and loved mercy? Even when woman in past ages has not herself been swift to shed blood, has not she inspired man to deeds of cruelty, and then, like Thais, —

"led the way
To light him to his prey"?

Is there not even a touch of cruelty in the nature of the otherwise gracious English Queen, which shows itself in her rigid insistence upon the rule which provides that, no matter what may be the state of the weather or the constitution of the individual, the ladies presented to her must exhibit uncovered shoulders in the sight of their sovereign?

The cruelty of man — for I am not asserting that man is not cruel

— springs from a motive which in itself is not to be altogether contemned. Ambition to a certain extent is a desirable possession, whether it manifests itself in a desire for power to be exercised for laudable ends or in a resolution to obtain wealth to a reasonable amount. It is the excess of ambition in its many forms which provokes man's cruelty.

Feminine cruelty is the outcome of less noble promptings, and, so it would seem, arises from indifference, vanity, or jealousy, according to its degree, — sometimes from a fusing of all three, — and it is seldom held in check by reason.

I wish that I might end here; for if this were all there were to urge, and I bring forward nothing that is new in this connection, the title of this essay might with some reason be termed unjust and its implied assumption declared too sweeping to be true; but, O you women who cry out upon the cruelty and selfishness of men; you who are defended from the storms of this world by the care of these rough men, and you who proudly defend yourselves without such aid; you who dwell as the daughters of kings, and you who fare as those to whom toil is no stranger; O you women who are virtuous and honest, why are your hearts steeled against those sisters of yours who stumbled on ways that seem smooth enough to you, who fell where you have walked upright?

Have you defended that sister of yours whose good name has been assailed as earnestly as you have rushed to the defence of your sex when you fancied it was slandered? Have you refused to believe evil of her against whom some stone has been cast? Have you refused to record your sentence against one accused till her guilt was absolutely sure? Have you not, when this last was proved, declared that guilt unpardonable and thrust the offender out from your life and from your thought forever? Have you ever stooped to help one of those who was weak where you were strong, or who was tempted when you were not, or who fell because the way to her was rougher than you have ever dreamed? Have you done all these things?

The judgments which man passes upon his fellows are tolerant where woman's are narrow, because, instead of the one aspect of the question which she perceives, he sees many: they are merciful where hers are cruel, because he recognizes more fully the stress of temptation and the complexity of motive which lead to transgression. There have been a few women who have helped their weaker sisters to rise when they had fallen, but they are indeed few. The majority of women have done what they could to keep those who are down still in that position. They have refused to believe in the possibility of reform: they have withdrawn from all contact with those who have once found temptation greater than they could bear; they have, by their inflexible attitude, made a return to virtue nearly impossible on the part of those who have once turned from it. Who should be tenderer toward a woman's sin than a virtuous woman, and who is harder? O you queens, who have with your virtuous hands thrust your weaker sisters still further in the mire; who have shown aversion where you might have shown mercy; who have hardened your hearts, that should have been soft with pity; who have turned coldly aside from these, your sisters, whom you might have saved, and gone your ways as though these were not; O you who have lifted from your heads the crown of gentleness and mercy that all your sex should wear, are you not, " ruthless " indeed.

THE BRUTAL SEX.

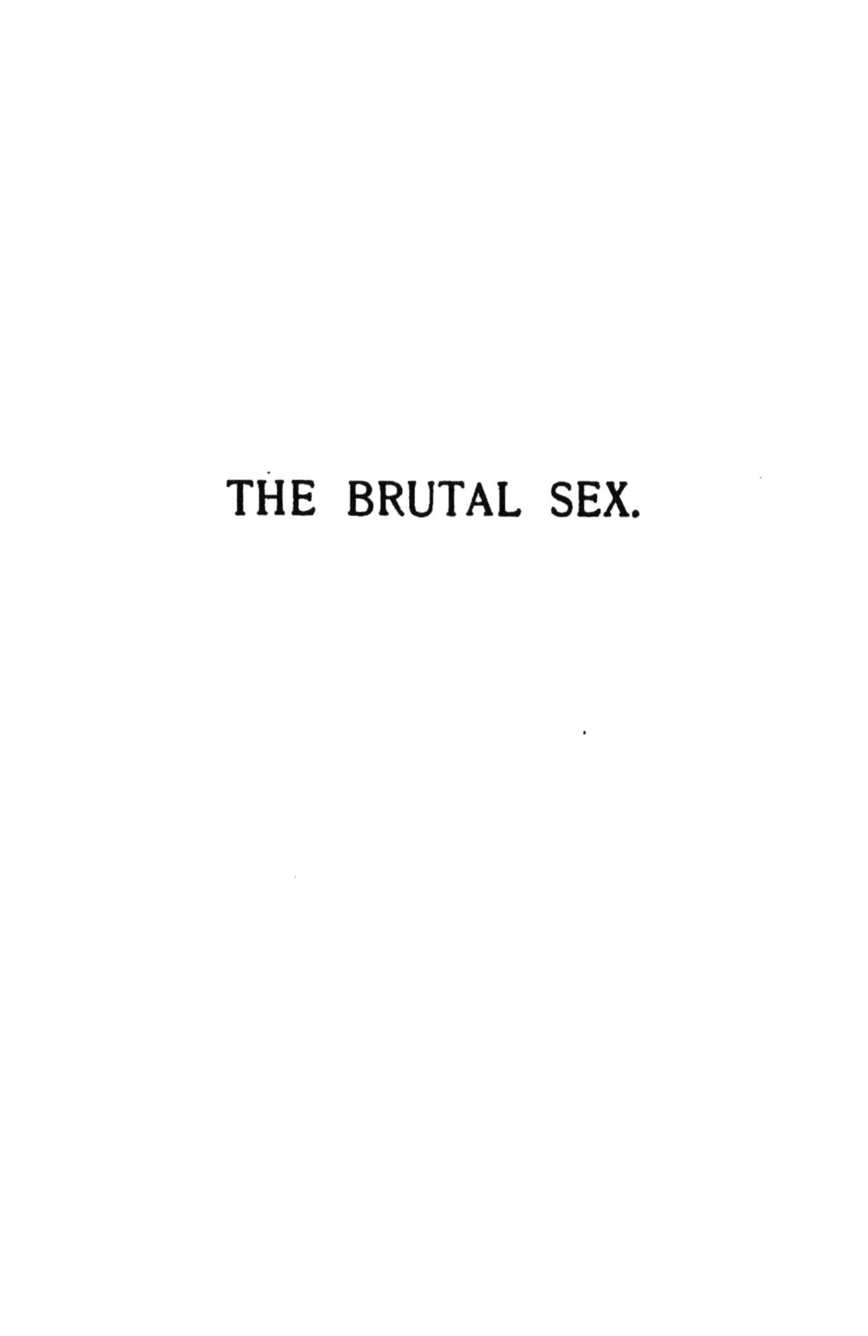

THE BRUTAL SEX.

＊＊＊＊

WHEN Mrs. Poyser, in the course of one of her memorable arguments with Mr. Craig on " the woman question," wound up by admitting that though women might be foolish, " God Almighty made ' em to match the men," she supplied a statement of the seemingly unanswerable variety which her sex have not been slow to make use of in discussions regarding the respective merits or failings of the sexes. As *Malvolio*, however,

when questioned concerning Pytha-
goras's assertion that the soul of
our grandam might haply inhabit a
bird, replied that he thought nobly
of the soul and in no way approved
of the opinion, so I must declare
that I think too nobly of woman to
approve altogether of Mrs. Poyser's
theory and assent to its proposition
that women were made to match
the men.   If it were true, then the
human race were in a most parlous
state.   If it were true, then the
masculine would not be *the brutal
sex.*

To be cruel is not necessarily to
be brutal, in the ordinary accepta-
tion of those terms, however lexicog-
raphers may decide the matter for
themselves.   A person may be both

brutal and cruel, or only cruel, or, again, only brutal. In ordinary speech we distinguish between the two words by applying the term "cruel" to merciless acts which seem to imply a definite amount of deliberate thought preparatory to their execution, and "brutal" to similar acts committed without such thought and on the impulse of the moment. So it is that we speak of "refined cruelty," but not of "refined brutality." I have elsewhere intimated that women are often cruel; I should be sorry to believe that they could be brutal.

Cruelty is a defensive attribute of weakness; brutality, the vice of strength. The exhibition of these two traits manifests itself early in our human nature. Let any one observe groups of boys and girls at their separate games, and he will see among the former the brute nature asserting its presence with more or less vehemence, according to circumstances, in a free interchange of kicks and blows, while among the girls he will observe actions that are cruel rather than brutal, and which involve mental rather than physical distress. But it is the brutal rather than the cruel side that comes into boldest relief. And among men and women the same degree of difference exists. The stronger sex is still the brutal one.

With brutality is often blended a vein of reckless generosity, a doubtful virtue, but the exercise of which often serves to moderate or even dissipate in the public mind the effect of the brutality. This, however, is somewhat aside from the main theme. It is not needful to go back to the past to sustain the assertion that the masculine sex, taken in its entirety, is a brutal one. We can find proofs enough of it close at hand in our own time. Nor need we take exaggerated instances of it, such as now and then shock us in Whitechapel atrocities or the acts of Stanley's rear-guard in darkest Africa, or in the practices of semi-barbarous peoples. We have but to look at existing states of things in the most enlightened nations of the globe.

Among the rougher elements that form part of the social structure, we find the most inhuman practices to be of common occurrence. The men think little of beating their beasts of burden most savagely, and nearly as often and as savagely, their unfortunate wives. The impulse to either act is very little restrained by reason, and is simply the result of an outbreak of brute nature.

If the brutality of modern life touched no greater extremes than these, and was confined to the lower strata of society, we might look for its elimination in time, for the progress of intelligence would supplement the workings of law. But brutality is deep-rooted in man's nature ; its impelling motives do not have their source in the accidents of the moment, when its most baleful consequences are con- cerned, but are among the funda- mental passions of man.

Think for a moment what is implied in the single fact that in no part of the world is it deemed safe for a woman to go alone after dark, unless, perhaps, in Japan, nor, in many localities, even by day. It is not enough to reply that woman must have a trustworthy masculine escort because she is timid. Why should she be timid? Under sim- ilar circumstances a man may fear the personal violence of an enemy or the loss of his money and valuables. A woman has to dread man's "wildness and the chances of the dark." In plain words, she fears that, if unattended, some man will seek to rob her of her honor. And is not this fear of hers a terrible arraignment of civilization itself? How much better does civilized man show above his savage brother in relation to this matter?

It may be urged that it is unfair to hold all men responsible for the lawlessness of a minority; yet what is this but to confess that the majority are powerless to restrain the minority, or to say that improvement in this regard is impossible? If in the vicinity of every large town in the United States there lurked a dozen or more fierce wolves that, after nightfall, went into the town and banqueted on such of the citizens as they could secure, we may without much doubt assert that such a state of things, when once found to exist, would come to a speedy termination; for each man would feel that the common safety of all demanded the exertion of his strength in the contest with the wild beasts. But let it be understood that the honor of every woman is endangered when she goes from place to place alone at night, and we accept the fact as no reproach on our common manhood, but merely fancy that all requirements of duty are satisfied if we provide defenceless woman with a responsible male escort.

But woman's timidity is an

inheritance, says some one. That is true enough; but is there no active present reason for its continued existence? Let any newspaper with its numberless accounts of brutal assaults upon women make answer to this. That the perpetrators of such crimes often meet with swift retributive justice at the hands of an enraged mob has little influence in the creation of a public opinion strong enough to make crimes of this kind eventually unknown, simply because public opinion, when it thus becomes the instrument of justice, is not worked upon by the nobler aspects of the case.

Crimes against property are always looked upon by the average man as more heinous than any others, and it is useless to deny that the average man regards his wife as his property. She is

"Something better than his dog, a little
    dearer than his horse,"

it is true, but his property nevertheless. The indignation which he feels on hearing of some assault upon a woman differs in degree, but scarcely in kind, from the horror with which certain frontier communities regard the crime of horse-stealing. In each case the sin is one which is committed against property. In the frontier town every man feels that his own property is in danger while the horse-thief is still at large; and similarly the average man argues with respect to his own wife while the ravisher goes unwhipped of justice. Hence his speedy resort to the swiftest punishment possible in each case.

But suppose the idea of personal ownership is not involved in any way, as it is, refine it how we may, in all instances of the kind first cited, or in all accusations of adultery brought by the husband against his wife. Suppose we consider simply one prominent attitude in which the majority of men stand towards womankind. And what is that attitude? Briefly and plainly it, is that man's physical welfare requires for its maintenance the moral ruin of unnumbered thousands of women.

It is prudery to be shocked at such a putting of the matter, when we know that the practice of the average man is in fullest accord with the statement just made. Our age is easily shocked in certain directions, but our superior virtue is not incontestably proved by the fact that we are less plain-spoken than our ancestors. What should concern us most is to see whether or no such a statement be true or false.

That it is a false or misleading presentment I leave for others to maintain; that it is a true condensation of the theory held by the majority of men I do not hesitate to assert.

The tolerant attitude taken by

many men of blameless lives towards sexual sins is often urged against them by women as a reproach.   In this particular women are partly right and partly wrong. They are in the wrong because they are prone to magnify the guilt of sins of this kind so far above that of other violations of the rule of right living, as thereby practically to ignore at times the existence of other sins. The seventh commandment is not the only one to be observed, nor is it any more binding than any of the others included in the decalogue.   They thus exhibit a distorted sense of proportion in morals, and so weaken the influence they might otherwise exert upon the practice of men in this direction. But they are in the right to a certain extent in urging their reproach because the easy judgment passed upon sexual sins, even by men who have no notion of committing them, helps in its way to make the commission of those offences more readily possible.

Masculine society tacitly assumes that the overwhelming majority of men will not remain virtuous. It also assumes that a vast number of women must lead unchaste lives in order that the sexual appetites of the before-mentioned men may be gratified. Now, see how differently the two sets of individuals involved in these assumptions are regarded by the world at large. The first-named are seeking the gratification of a natural instinct, we say. If the men are young and unmarried, we say " Boys will be boys," and if married, we are not very much inclined to severer judgment so long as there is no outraging of conventionalities. But if young women indulge in immoral practices, we do not good-naturedly excuse them by saying " Girls will be girls," or extend to them the same leniency of judgment passed upon their brothers : what is natural in the one sex therefore appears to be considered most perverse and unnatural in the other. We forgive the one class readily enough, or even deny the need of the exercise of forgiveness ; the other class we refuse to respect, if we be men, or, if we be women, we refuse to forgive.

To tacitly admit that incontinence is, if not commendable, at least a very venial transgression for the male sex, but something quite opposite for the other sex, carries with it the practical confession that right thinking as well as right acting in relation to so important a matter is for the present unattainable. It is to admit, moreover, that man has made but very little progress from the animal to the spiritual in this respect, in all the ages that have gone before up to the present, and it seemingly involves the denial of the possibility of such advance in the future.

The church has not contributed materially to the solution of this moral question. It has held up an ideal of what man should be in this respect, but it has never strenuously denied what the practice of the average man declares, namely, that the attainment of such an ideal of virtue by man is an impossible achievement. It has *preached* chastity for man as well as for woman, but it has usually stopped at the preaching. The prayer-book rubric provides that any clergyman may refuse communion to a " notorious evil liver" until "he hath openly declared himself to have truly repented and amended his former naughty life;" but how often do we find a clergyman brave enough to insist that the provisions of this rubric shall be carried out?

It matters little what advancement is made in any or all departments of human knowledge, or what increase of refinement marks our progress through the centuries, if men are to remain at the end of it all as essentially brutal in the satisfaction of sexual desire as the savage in his wilderness countless æons ago. So long as the average man, refined or otherwise, persists in acting up to his belief that the physical well-being of his sex inexorably calls for the separation from the ranks of virtuous women of hundreds of thousands of their sisters, and the consequent moral ruin of these ministers to his pleasure; so

long as he contentedly suffers this
perpetual sacrifice to be offered up
in his behalf, so long may ours be
truthfully as well as sadly called the
brutal sex!

"OUR DREADFUL AMERICAN MANNERS"

"OUR DREADFUL AMERICAN MANNERS"

*** * * ***

I QUOTE the phrase. The most of us have heard it, and have repelled the implication it contains with more or less vigor, according to the strength of our convictions upon the subject.

"We should like to know," say some impulsive patriots, "whether American manners are not just as good as German or Italian manners, for example. Why, when we were staying at Lucerne one summer, we used to witness most shocking exhibitions of bad manners from the

German and Italian tourists — yes, and from those of other nations too."

No doubt you did, my dear patriots; but what has that to do with the matter? Upon this subject we may ask, as an American politician is once said to have exclaimed upon a very different topic, " What have we to do with abroad ? " That there is such a thing as Russian or German ill-breeding does not absolve Americans from responsibility for their own manners. We shall never reform ourselves by comparing ourselves with others to their disadvantage.

The presence of bad manners necessarily implies the existence of a standard from which divergence has been made. That standard is established by a minority of persons trained to habits of thoughtfulness and usefulness. How small that minority is, a very little experience will demonstrate, and we do not always find its members just where we should naturally look for them.

One might suppose that in congressional and legislative halls we should find a high standard of manners constantly preserved; but the honorable gentlemen who fill them have quite other views as to what constitutes their duty to their constituents, unless, indeed, they instruct on the principle of showing what is to be avoided by those who wish to be considered well-bred.

It is not so long ago that a large

number of Columbia College students broke up a theatrical performance by their outrageous behavior
in the theatre. True, they were
young men, and it is the fashion to
excuse much to youth ; but the
majority of them came from homes
of refinement, and better things
might reasonably have been ex-
pected of them. If we are not to
look for good manners among the
men who are trained in the fore-
most colleges and universities, where
are we to look for them?

Perhaps at no time in our natural
life have the tokens of external
polish been more general than at
present ; that is, there are a greater
number of people than ever before,
who lift the hat in salutation, who

have fairly good table manners, who respect the finger-bowl on its merits, and keep the knife in proper subjection to its mate, the fork; but the native savagery is only partially obscured. Watch the procession of people leaving the dining-room of a summer hotel, each industriously plying his toothpick. Observe the rows of spittoons which are displayed in railway cars, hotel parlors and corridors, steamboat saloons, public halls, and business offices. Observe the well-dressed man with his cigar and the laborer with his pipe. Is the one, with his presumed advantages of training, one whit more regardful of the comfort of persons near him than the other, who has not had these advantages? Note the behavior of the knot of friends who are going on an excursion together. If they are men, they puff their cigars in calm disregard of persons near them on the steamer's deck, and oblige every one within hearing distance to listen to their loud and jovial conversation. If they are women, they talk at the tops of their voices and generally in concert, and involuntary listeners are made conversant with that host of minute details amid which the feminine mind delights to wander. If the party be made up of men and women, there is a still greater confusion of tongues, much good-nature, a great deal of joking carried on in a high key, while the amount of decorum manifested depends upon the social position of the members composing the party. This is a variable quantity, however, and the blue blood is not always an assurance of absolute propriety.

Urban manners are supposed to be superior to rustic ones, but the superiority extends only to externals. It may be safely said that not more than one person in a hundred in a city street shows any consideration for his neighbor. The plain fact is, that very few of us care what opinion our neighbor is forming of us. Independence is a good thing, but it soon passes the boundaries of good taste and good feeling and becomes noisy self-assertiveness.

The rule of finest manners or-

dains that in a public place two or
more persons engaged in conversation should not obtrude that conversation upon the ears of disinter-
ested third parties.   Because A has
met B in the street, it is not needful that C and D should be obliged
to listen to what A and B have to
say to each other.   Nor when Mrs.
E meets Mrs. F in the street-car,
should these two estimable matrons
take all the other occupants of the
car into their confidence respecting
what interests the two friends only.
There is no rule of good breeding
oftener violated than this.   Go
where one will, its observance can
hardly ever be noted — its violation
is almost universal.   The woman
who calls across the alley to her

neighbor leaning from the opposite tenement - house window is no greater a sinner in this respect than the fine lady who discusses with a companion, at the entrance of a theatre or a church, topics which are of interest only to herself and her friend, but which every one near her is obliged to hear. It is not that they mean to be heard by persons about them : *it is that they do not care.*

" I don't say anything I am ashamed of," says Simplicitas; " anybody is welcome to know what I am talking about."

True ; but has the outside world no rights that Simplicitas is bound to respect ? Why should Quietas, on his way down the street, be

obliged to listen to all that Simplicitas, just in front of him, is pouring
into the ears of his friend? Simplicitas may be quoting from the ante-
Nicene fathers, but that is no reason
why Quietas should be forced into
the unwilling position of listener.

Perhaps Simplicitas may urge
that his voice is one that cannot be
pitched on a key low enough to be
heard only by the person he is
addressing. That is a misfortune,
to be sure; but if he cannot learn
to modulate his voice out of consideration for others, he must keep
silent in public. There is no other
course open to him.

It is the custom in some liturgi-
cal churches for the congregation
to remain in silent prayer for a

moment after the benediction. From the point of view of decorum and good breeding, there is something to be said for the practice; but surely there can be no legitimate defence urged for the custom which prevails in non-liturgical churches of using the moment of benediction as a season of preparation for leaving. Persons who take this time for putting on their overshoes, getting into their overcoats, or groping for their hats and canes *are distinctly ill-bred*, whether they are members of mission churches or worship beneath gorgeous "roofs of plaster painted like an Indian squaw."

People who occupy the middle seats in the rows of chairs in a theatre do not afford the best ex-

ample possible of their good manners when they oblige their neigh-
bors to rise in order to let them
pass backward and forward between
the acts of the play. And persons
who, in order to "avoid the crowd,"
leave the theatre or concert-room a
few moments before the conclusion
of the performance, and by the confusion attending their departure
spoil the effect of the last scene of
the play or the closing number of
the concert, are quite as flagrant
offenders against the code of good
manners.

It is a common complaint of
ushers at church weddings that it
is very difficult to reserve for the
invited guests the seats which have
been set aside for them. A mob of

well-dressed women, intent upon securing good seats, press past the ushers, in very many cases, establish themselves comfortably in the reserved seats, and will not be ousted therefrom.

In the railway trains the majority of the passengers seem bent upon retaining in their possession one more seat than they have paid for, even when they see that other persons are thereby obliged to stand.

Everywhere one meets with self-assertion. Sometimes it is aggressive and conscious; sometimes it is passive and unconscious; but always and ever it is based upon the principle that the comfort of the many must be sacrificed to that of the individual. We stand and talk with a friend in the middle of a crowded pavement, and it matters very little if we thereby obstruct the stream of travel ; we make our sidewalks and the floors of our public halls filthy with tobacco juice; we smoke in the street, and almost everywhere else, in the presence of non-smokers ; we flourish our toothpicks in public ; we commit not only these, but ten thousand other sins against good manners ; and then we are surprised if any one calls us an ill-bred people. Perhaps we are not ill-bred when compared with certain other peoples ; but we have no business to so compare ourselves. The only standard by which to measure ourselves is that established by the practice of the thoughtful, unselfish minority — a practice which consists in doing nothing to promote individual comfort, pleasure, or convenience that shall interfere with the comfort or well-being (in the broad sense of the term) of those about us.

" Manners," says Emerson, " form the cloak that virtue wears when she goes abroad ; " and lest our virtue be taken for other than it is, it becomes us to see that there are no rents or gaping holes in this outer garment of ours.

The plain, unpalatable fact must be stated, that in spite of the presence among us of many persons whose lives are regulated by a spirit of the finest, most thoughtful courtesy, as a people we Americans are noisy, boastful, aggressive, glorying in our " push " and self-assertiveness, and quite content that these most disagreeable features of our national character should obscure our better and nobler qualities which lie beneath.

I am not concerned with the causes which have produced the results complained of. I am speaking of present facts — facts which are not now brought up for notice for the first time, but have received adverse comment before. But the most serious aspect of the matter is the spirit of indifference to reform which is practically manifested in the common belief that we are better bred than the majority of nations. So long as we are satisfied with ourselves there will be no progress.

But we are not a stupid people, and we are still somewhat sensitive to foreign strictures upon our manners and customs. We have been known to resent foreign criticism in past years and then apply ourselves to reform what was criticised.

Let us be as resentful as we will, and abuse to our heart's content the insolent foreigner or the unpatriotic native who says that there are some very weak places in our armor, and then let us confess to ourselves that our armor *is* weak, and take counsel of our better and unselfish selves how it may be mended. Then, and not till then, shall we cease to hear of " our dreadful American manners."